THE HITCHHIKER

AN EROTIC ADVENTURE

VICTORIA RUSH

VOLUME 24

JADE'S EROTIC ADVENTURES - BOOK 24

COPYRIGHT

The Hitchhiker © 2020 Victoria Rush

Cover Design © 2020 PhotoMaras

All Rights Reserved

FEEL THE RUSH:

Jade's Erotic Adventures – Book 1

When lonely divorcée Jade seeks to broaden her horizons, she's invited to a private dinner event which promises to stimulate all of her senses. Wearing nothing but masquerade masks, dinner guests receive special service under the table while their fellow diners look on...

The Dinner Party

Jade's Erotic Adventures - Book 2

Jade discovers an exotic adventure club where strangers meet to explore each other's bodies in mysterious dark rooms. Using special effects to project swirling light patterns onto their figures, the shifting shadows provide just enough illumination to highlight their naked bodies while protecting their identities...

The Dark Room

Jade's Erotic Adventures - Book 3

Jade discovers a yoga club where members stretch and explore each other's bodies in the buff. She books an appointment, and during the first session meets a young redhead who tantalizes her with her flexibility and stunning body...

Naked Yoga

For the uninhibited...

1

———

I'd been looking forward to this trip for weeks. Normally, I flew to client meetings this far from home, but Des Moines was only four hours away by car. Factoring in check-in time at the airport, going through security, and taking taxis on both ends, it would take at least that long to travel there by plane. Plus, driving was infinitely less hassle. All I had to do was jump in my SUV, turn on the nav system, and point my way to my destination. All while soaking up the pretty midwestern scenery and listening to my favorite tunes on the radio.

Besides, I hadn't been on a road trip in years, and I was looking forward to feeling the sun on my face and the wind in my hair. There was something strangely romantic and liberating about the call of the open road. Being able to stop whenever you wanted, take a little detour if the mood struck, and watching the intoxicating flow of traffic like so many ants scurrying over their anthill.

After packing up a few days' worth of provisions and locking up my house, I turned out of my subdivision onto Route 30, heading west. This part of the trip was still familiar from my childhood forays into the lake district of northern Wisconsin, and I smiled as I breathed in the pastoral landscape of the passing farms. The countryside was a brilliant patchwork of yellows and greens, and my head lolled from side to side as I followed the neatly arranged rows of corn, soybeans, and wheat while my car glided down the two-lane highway.

After glancing down to dial in my favorite country music station, I looked up to see an unusual sight on the side of the road a few hundred feet ahead. It was something I hadn't seen for a long time–a hitchhiker. Curious to see who was still daring enough to catch a ride from a stranger in these troubling times, I squinted as the traveler came into focus. As the distance between us closed, my eyes widened when I realized it was a girl.

A young, scantily clad girl.

I could hardly believe my eyes as my car rushed past her. She couldn't have been more than eighteen years old, if that. Wearing tight, cut-off jean shorts and a white tank top, she had the young, nubile figure of a high-school teenager. My first reaction was one of shock and disbelief.

What in God's name is a girl like that doing thumbing a ride on the highway? Doesn't she realize how many predators are out there looking for an easy mark just like her?

As I watched her get smaller and smaller in my rear-view mirror, I shook my head disapprovingly, then suddenly screeched on the brakes and pulled over onto the shoulder. Normally I wouldn't give a second thought to taking on a hitchhiker knowing there was just as much risk for the driver, especially for a single woman like me. But there was something about this girl that I couldn't resist. Whether it was her naïve vulnerability or the appearance of her slender brown legs, I wasn't sure. Either way, the little twitch in my pussy told me this was an opportunity I couldn't pass up.

At first, she didn't notice that I'd pulled over, since I was so far ahead of her. I honked my horn and flashed my lights and she turned her head in my direction, then she picked up her small suitcase and began jogging toward me. Feeling sorry for her, I put my car in reverse and slowly backed up along the shoulder until we closed the gap. When she came up on my right side, I rolled down the passenger window and peered out at her.

"Where are you headed?" I smiled.

"California," she said, catching her breath.

"I'm only going as far as Des Moines, but I'm happy to point you in the right direction."

"Thanks," she nodded.

I unlocked my doors and tilted my head toward the back seat.

"You can throw your bag in the back if you want. But there's a lot more room up front to stretch your legs."

The girl opened the rear door and threw her carry-on-size roller bag on the back seat then climbed in the front next to me.

I smiled at her and checked my driver's mirror, then slowly pulled back onto the highway.

"I'm Jade," I said, introducing myself.

"Brooklyn," the girl replied.

"That's a pretty name. Do you go by Brooke, or Lynn, or do you like to be called by your full name?"

"Either way is fine. But most of my friends call me Brooke."

"Brooke it is," I nodded, interested to learn more about this mysterious stranger. "So, *California*? What's taking a pretty girl like you so far away from home?"

"I dunno," she said. "Just spreading my wings, I guess. Now that I've finished high school, I figured I might as well try my luck in La-La Land."

"Are you looking to be a movie star?" I laughed.

"Probably not. I thought I'd get a job as a waitress and check things out. But you never know, right? Wasn't that how Marilyn Monroe got discovered?"

I glanced over at the girl and smiled. With her curly blonde hair and piercing blue eyes, she could easily pass for a younger version of the matinee idol.

"Actually, I think she was working in a factory. But with those all-American looks, you've got as good a chance as any."

"Thanks," the girl said.

For the next couple of minutes, awkward silence filled the car as Brooke peered out her side of the window at the passing fields.

"It's pretty this time of the year, isn't it?" I said, making small talk. "I always like going for a drive as we approach harvest time. The crops are nearing full bloom, and you can smell the perfume in the air. Do you mind if I open the sunroof a bit so we can soak up the sunshine?"

"By all means," she said. "I probably should start working on my tan so I can keep up with all those California golden girls."

"I don't think you've got much to worry about," I said, glancing at her tawny thighs poking out of her cut-off jeans. There were so many questions I still had about this shy beauty. "But you're awfully young to be pulling up stakes and heading to the other side of the country. What do your parents think of this idea?"

"I'm not sure they much *care*," she shrugged. "My father lives in New York and my mother shacked up with an alcoholic who only seems to care where his next drink is coming from."

"I'm sorry to hear," I said, wincing at the thought of this pretty girl being neglected by uncaring parents.

"It's cool," she said. "I'm free as a bird now and the world is my oyster."

I peered over at Brooke, noticing her body language didn't match her cavalier attitude. She had her arms crossed tightly over her chest while her foot tapped nervously against the floorboard.

"Do they even *know* where you're headed?" I said. "I'm sorry to sound like an overbearing mother, but I'd hate for them to worry what happened to you."

"We had a fight earlier in the week when I told them I was thinking of leaving. My mother wanted me to go to college and my step-father just sees me as his meal ticket. I think he was afraid if I left that my mother wouldn't have any reason to keep him around."

I glanced over at Brooke and noticed a faint bruise around the base of her neck.

"But you *are* eighteen though? I mean, I wouldn't want to get either one of us in trouble..."

"Yes," she huffed sarcastically. "Just turned. I got the hell out of there just in time."

"Do you mind my asking why you weren't interested in going to college? You seem like a smart, well-spoken girl. Weren't your grades good enough?"

"I did well enough in high school," she said. "I just wanted to spread my wings before I get locked into another four years of school and a boring, dead-end job."

I couldn't help admire her free spirit and sense of adventure. But I wondered if there was another reason for her sudden uprooting.

"And there's nothing *else* keeping you close to home? Boyfriends, a steady job..."

"I've been saving up from my weekend job at Applebee's these last two years. Now I've finally got enough to start over on the west coast. I've had plenty enough of boys. They're only interested in one thing anyhow."

I felt my heart racing, seeing a window of opportunity opening. While I was in no hurry to take advantage of her, I felt like I'd found a kindred spirit. Even though there was fifteen years separating us in age, we shared a similar view on life with neither of us wanting to be held back by society's norms.

"Yeah, I know what you mean. My first husband wasn't exactly Mr. Perfect either. I'm in no hurry to jump into bed with another guy anytime soon."

I noticed Brooke's body language beginning to relax as she placed her arm on the door rest for support, hunching down a few inches in her seat.

"What are you headed to Des Moines for?" she asked.

"A meeting with a client. I'm a graphic designer and I'm going to review some ideas he had for updating his corporate identity."

"Corporate identity?"

"He operates a chain of restaurants. He wants to refresh his logo, menus, signage, and so on. It's a branding thing."

"Mmm," Brooke nodded. "Will you be staying long?"

"It's just a one-day meeting. But I've booked a hotel overnight so I'll be fresh for the drive back tomorrow."

Brooke peered back out the side of her window as we listened to the sound of the wind whistling through the overhead sunroof and soft country music on the radio. Periodically, I'd catch her stealing glimpses out the side of her eyes at my legs in my tight jeans and my loose blouse flapping in the breeze.

"Do you like your job?" she asked after a few minutes.

"It's a living," I said. "At least I'm my own boss and I get to exercise my creative juices. Each commission is different and I meet some interesting people along the way. How about you? Do you have any special passions or talents?"

"Not really. I was pretty good at science and math at school, but I can't think of a job in either of those fields that interests me."

I nodded my head, trying to think of a way to get her to open up a little more. So far, she'd played her cards pretty close to the vest, and I was beginning to wonder if there was any way I could draw her out of her shell.

"There's a lot you can do with those skills," I said. "Especially if you go on to college. Quite a few math majors move into finance. Quants make some big bucks on Wall Street. Trading, risk management, investment banking–maybe it would be an opportunity for you to reconnect with your father in New York?"

"He's got his own life now with a new bride and two toddlers. I'm not sure there's much room for me in his picture any longer."

"What about science?" I frowned. "There's so many interesting careers you could explore in that area. Marine biology, space exploration, you could even be a doctor."

"I'm too young to be thinking about all that mature stuff," Brooke said. "I've got my whole life ahead of me. There'll be plenty of time to explore my options when I settle down."

I peered over at Brooke, watching the breeze from the open sunroof swirling her blonde locks against her pretty face as she leaned back, closing her eyes.

"Sorry, I'm sure the last thing you want right now is to be stuck on a four-hour road trip with someone who sounds like your mother. No more career counseling, I promise. Let's just enjoy the open road and the wind in our hair!"

She issued a smile of relief, then I noticed her tapping her fingers on the edge of the door as she peered outside.

"Do you like Blake Shelton?" I said, seeing her foot tapping in rhythm to the music on the radio.

"He's fun to watch on The Voice. But I like this song. He and Gwen look like they really love each other in the video version."

"It sure is dreamy," I said, turning up the volume. "I'm not sure I'll ever find that kind of love."

While we listened to the song, Brooke began to hum the melody quietly under her breath.

"*I don't wanna look back in thirty years,*" I sang along to the lyrics, trying to get her to open up. "And wonder who I'm married to..."

"*Wanna say it now, wanna make it clear,*" Brooke joined in softly. "*For only you and God to hear...*"

"*When you love someone,*" we joined in together, "*they say you set 'em free. But that ain't gonna work for me...*"

As the drumbeat introduced the chorus, I turned the volume up higher.

"*I don't wanna live without you,*" we both belted. "*I don't wanna even breathe, don't wanna dream about you, wanna wake up with you next to me.*"

Brooke had a sweet, lilting tone, but I could see sadness in her eyes as she sang along with me. I smiled at her as I cranked the volume up until the beat surrounded us in the pounding cabin.

"*I don't wanna go down any other road now,*" she sang, looking back at me. "*I don't wanna love nobody but you.*"

"Looking in your eyes now," we sang together. *"If I had to die now, I don't wanna love nobody but you..."*

As the song drifted off to the second verse, Brooke peered out her window, singing the rest of the song to herself. When I glanced over at her, I realized how vulnerable and alone she must have felt. I had no idea what kind of hardships she'd experienced in her young life, but from the pining sound of her voice, she looked broken and lost.

I peered ahead and saw a sign for a roadside rest area and looked over at her.

"Are you hungry?" I said. "There's an A&W restaurant at the pull-off. Nothing like a burger and fries with a down-home root beer to drown out your sorrows. My treat."

"Sure," Brooke said, smiling back at me. "I could go for a root beer right about now."

As I pulled off into the rest area, my heart skipped a beat. Somehow I knew this trip was going to have a lot more twists and turns than I planned.

2

Brooke and I went inside the restaurant and waited in line while we decided what we wanted from the display menu behind the counter. I noticed a group of teenage boys in an adjacent line ogling her figure while they snickered and elbowed each other playfully. Whether they chose to keep their distance because they were too afraid to approach her or because they thought I was her mother, I wasn't sure.

But for the first time since I'd met her, I saw her up close from head to toe. Her ass was firm and well rounded, with the tight seam of her cut-off shorts separating her buttocks into two perfect circular globes. Her breasts weren't large, but they sat up prominently on her chest, pointing out like two snow cones under her form-fitting tank top. Her skin was soft and dewy like a teenager's, and golden brown with not a blemish to be found anywhere on her slender arms and legs.

As I admired her youthful, girl-next-door good looks, I understood why half the eyes in the room were checking her out.

If I was a teenage boy, I'd want a piece of that ass too.

I moved protectively beside her, and after we placed our order and collected our food trays, I found a booth in the far corner of the room. As she dug into her bacon and cheese burger, I watched the movement of her face while she peered back at me.

"What?" she said, gulping down her first mouthful. "Have I got mustard on my face or something?"

"No," I chuckled. "I was just thinking how a pretty girl dressed in such a skimpy outfit figured she could safely hitchhike her way all across the country."

"I don't know," she shrugged. "I've never done it before. But I figured the more skin I showed, the quicker I'd get picked up."

"That's for sure," I said, noticing the boys seated on the other side of the restaurant still stealing glances at her. "But you must know how attractive you are and how vulnerable you'd be to somebody who might have ulterior motives."

"I never really thought much about it, I guess," she said, dipping one of her fries in the cup of ketchup. "I was in such a hurry to get the hell out of my current abusive home, I just packed my bag and left."

"Is that what happened to your neck?" I said, glancing down at her bruise.

Brooke sat back on the bench and peered out the window pensively.

"My mom's boyfriend grabbed me there when I threatened to leave. Par for the course with that asshole."

I glanced at her and furrowed my brow, wondering what other indignities she'd suffered at the hands of the abusive lush.

"Did he abuse you in any *other* ways?"

"He tried often enough, but I got pretty good at reading

the signs when he had too much to drink. I just made myself scarce until he sobered up."

"Now I see why you were so eager to leave," I nodded. "But you have to be careful that you don't trade one dangerous caretaker for another. There are a lot of ill-intentioned people out there just looking for an easy mark like yourself."

"I can take care of myself," she said. "I've made it this far on my own."

"Well, technically, you're less than one tenth of the way to Shangri La Land," I chuckled. "You've still got a long road ahead of you."

Brooke dipped another french fry into her ketchup, drawing some circles on the paper placemat lining her tray.

"As long as I'm careful whose car I get into, everything should be okay, right? There must be *lots* of other nice people like you out there willing to help a girl out."

"I suppose so, but you're rolling the dice with every new pick-up. It's unlikely you're going to find one person who'll take you the entire way."

"Maybe," she said, noisily sipping her root beer through her straw to distract attention from the conversation. "But tell me more about you. Do you have kids? Where do you live? Do you have any special plans for the future?"

"No kids," I laughed. "We barely had enough time to get started before our marriage disintegrated. I live in Naperville, just outside Chicago. As for the future, I'm just taking it day by day."

"You're not far from where *I* used to live in Aurora," Brooke said. "We're almost neighbors. What happened to your marriage, if you don't mind my asking. Why was it so short?"

"He wasn't very–*attentive*–to my needs," I said. "I guess it just wasn't everything I thought it was cracked up to be. You know, the knight in shining armor and all that."

"Like in that movie Pretty Woman?"

"Ha," I laughed, almost choking on my drink. "It was slightly different circumstances, but yeah, I guess I was expecting someone to sweep me off my feet and take me away to his castle to live happily ever after."

"No *other* worthy candidates since then?"

"I'm not really looking for that kind of relationship anymore. Like you said–I've had my fill of boys."

"Mmm," Brooke nodded, glancing down at the cleavage in my open blouse as she took another sip of her root beer.

For the rest of our lunch date, we teased each other about our inept experiences with men, giggling amongst ourselves at the juvenile attempts of the boys across the room trying to attract her attention. When we finished our meal, we skipped out into the parking lot holding hands, then we jumped in the car and cranked up the music, wailing together over the corny country songs. The time passed quickly, and before I knew it, I saw the interchange approaching to exit into Des Moines.

"Listen," I said, glancing at the clock on my dashboard. "I don't feel right about just dropping you off at the side of the highway. Why don't you come with me while I check into my hotel before I head off to see my client? You can freshen up and watch a movie until I get back. Then we can have dinner and you're welcome to stay with me overnight before heading back out on the road tomorrow."

"Okay," Brooke said, nodding her head gently. "Thank you for everything. For lunch, for picking me up–and for being such a good listener. I can't imagine I'll find anyone who's half as much fun as you to spend the rest of my trip with."

"Don't give it a second thought," I said, smiling back at her warmly. "This has been an unexpected surprise for me too. You've made my boring trip to Des Moines so much more interesting."

I took the second exit and drove to the downtown Marriott, then I ordered a room with two double beds, and we carried our light bags inside. After changing into my business clothes and straightening up my lipstick and mascara, I handed Brooke one of the two room keys I'd been given at the front desk.

"I shouldn't be more than a couple of hours," I said. "Why don't you make yourself comfortable while I'm away. Feel free to order a movie and charge any meals to the room. But whatever you do, stay far away from the single men you find in the hotel. You'd be the perfect distraction while they're away from their wives back home."

"Don't worry," Brooke laughed. "I'll stay right here until you get back. Good luck at your meeting."

"Thanks, hun," I smiled. "See you soon."

For the rest of the afternoon, I had a hard time concentrating at my meeting with my client. All I could think about was Brooke's pretty face and the look she gave me when I left the room. Even though there was a wide gulf in age between the two of us, I found myself strangely attracted to the free-spirited girl and I was eager to get back to her as quickly as I could. I felt much more than a mother-and-daughter-type bond; my head was spinning and my stomach had butterflies, like I had a teenage crush. Which I suppose it *was*, in a strangely perverted way. Although the periodic twitching in my pussy told me this was a decidedly *grown-up* infatuation.

When my client invited me out for dinner at the close of our meeting, I politely declined, using the excuse of wanting to visit family members in town. I rushed back to my hotel, hoping Brooke hadn't gotten second thoughts about staying with me for the evening, as I fumbled awkwardly with my room key outside the hotel room door. When I swung it open, I was relieved to see her sitting upright on one of the beds, watching the movie Pretty Woman while munching on a large bag of Cheesies.

"I was afraid maybe you wouldn't *be* here when I got back," I said, throwing my briefcase on the opposite bed.

"Of course I'd be here," she said. "Why would I throw away this free meal ticket?"

I glanced at the TV and smiled.

"I see you've made yourself comfortable. Have you been fantasizing about finding your knight in shining armor?"

"Maybe," she said. "Although Richard Gere isn't exactly my type."

"Oh?" I said, hoping to get more hints about her sexual persuasion. "Who *is* your type?"

"I dunno," she said. "I'm still figuring it out. But it seems to be rapidly morphing away from the Tom Cruise leading man prototype."

"He's too short for you anyhow," I laughed, recognizing a familiar scene in her movie. "I love this part when Richard Gere's character pulls up in his stretch limousine and begs Julia Roberts to run away with him."

Brooke peered up at me then patted the bed beside her.

"Why don't you come join me while we finish the movie together? Do you like Cheesies?"

I laughed as I kicked off my leather pumps and threw my suit jacket on the bed.

"I haven't had them in ages, but yeah, they used to be one of my favorite guilty pleasures."

I plopped myself down on the bed beside Brooke, and we watched the rest of the movie side-by-side as we noisily crunched on the cheesy snack. When it was finally over, we looked at our orange-crusted fingers and giggled.

"*Ew,*" Brooke said, scrunching up her face. "I can't believe we ate that whole bag in one sitting. I've got to wash myself up before I get this all over everything."

While Brooke disappeared into the washroom, I cleaned my hands with wet wipes from my purse, then I changed out of my work clothes back into my jeans. When she emerged a few minutes later, she peered at my new ensemble and smiled.

"I like this look better on you," she said. "You look less like my mother and more like my partner-in-crime."

"Like *Thelma and Louise*?" I smiled. "God forbid that I'd remind you of your mother."

"I don't think there's any danger of that," she said, checking my figure out like I was with her at the restaurant.

"Are you up for a proper dinner after eating all that junk food?" I said, changing the subject. "I could go for a nice steak and a glass of wine right about now."

"Absolutely," Brooke said. "Although I'll have to pass on the wine, unless Iowa has a lower drinking age than Illinois."

"Oh yeah," I said. "I keep forgetting how young you are. I'm sure we can find something else to keep you amused. Maybe they can scare up a Shirley Temple or something like that."

"Ha!" Brooke said, placing her hands on her hips in mock protest. "I'm not *that* young!"

We took the elevator down to the lobby, then I asked at the front desk for the location of some good nearby restaurants. After enquiring about Brooke's food preferences, we decided on the Outback Steakhouse. When we were seated at the restaurant, I ordered a top sirloin steak with a glass of cabernet and Brooke ordered the pork ribs and a Coke. As we dug into our meals and talked about our favorite movies, I kept staring at Brooke's pretty face smeared with BBQ sauce, imagining it was my pussy juices instead of the tangy marinade.

"You're giving me that *look* again," she said, noticing me staring at her lips.

"It's just that you seem to have a propensity for finger food and getting your fingers messy while you eat."

"Hey, I'm a *teenager!*" she protested. "You can go ahead and eat your old-people food all prim and proper with a knife and fork. I'm gonna enjoy my pizza and burgers and fried food all I like."

"Who are you calling *old*?" I said, raising an eyebrow.

"Well you're older than *me*, aren't you? You've already been married and divorced, holding down a boring day job, driving an old person car–"

"It's not an *old person's* car," I said. "And I'm not boring, I'm just–*responsible*. Something you'd do well to learn before you end up living in the streets or get picked up by some sugar daddy."

"I didn't *ask* for all this," she said, twirling her finger sarcastically in the air while peering around the restaurant. "I was doing just *fine* before you plucked me off the highway."

I swallowed my mouthful with a lump in my throat as I

digested what had just happened. Somehow, we'd gone from laughing about our favorite movies to disparaging each other's life choices. My heart began racing a million miles an hour, shocked that we'd had our first fight after barely knowing each other for one day.

For the rest of the meal and the drive back to the hotel, we hardly said a word to one another as we stared out our windows, fuming. But the tightness in my stomach told me this was more than just a minor quarrel. People didn't get this passionate about issues and this angry at one another unless there was already some strong feelings between them. But mostly, I was afraid that I'd lost Brooke and that she'd use this as an excuse to run away again.

When we got back to the hotel, we took the elevator silently back up to our room then Brooke kicked off her sneakers, pulled her bra out from under her tank top and she climbed under the covers of her bed, sulking. I took a few minutes to brush my teeth and remove my makeup, then I pulled on a t-shirt and got into my bed wearing only my panties. As we both lay on the bed staring up at the ceiling, we could hear each other breathing mere inches away.

My mind raced thinking about what I should do with this young girl who'd I'd grown so close to in such a short period of time. I dreaded the idea of driving back home tomorrow without her, but I was far more worried about her continuing on her way by herself. After this new flare-up, I began to wonder if it wasn't for the best for the two of us to part company cleanly.

After a long pause, Brooke was the first to break the silence.

"I'm sorry, Jade, she said. "I didn't mean what I said about you being old and boring. I actually think you're one of the coolest, prettiest, and smartest persons I've met in a long time."

I paused for a long moment, feeling my heartbeat returning to normal.

"And I didn't mean what I said about your being irresponsible. I admire your free spirit and independence. I wish I were as courageous as you when I was your age."

For the next two hours, we talked about our dreams and aspirations, joking about our lost loves and missed opportunities. By the time I drifted off to sleep, I felt much more comfortable about the strength of our fledgling relationship. But a few hours later, I woke to the sound of rustling next to me in the pitch black. Brooke was shifting her weight erratically under her bedsheets, and I held my breath trying to listen to what she was doing.

After a few minutes, it became apparent from her raspy breathing and the rhythmic rustling of her sheets that she was masturbating under the covers. I could hardly believe what I was hearing, and my panties filled with moistness as I got more and more turned on listening to her pleasuring herself. She tried to be as quiet as she could, but the unmistakable ratcheting of her breath and the faster rustling of her sheets left little doubt that she was nearing climax. Suddenly, I could see her lifting her hips off the bed in the soft moonlight filtering through the crack in our curtains while she gasped in staccato succession.

Fuck me, I thought, squeezing my thighs together quietly under my covers. *That is the hottest thing I've ever heard in my life.*

I wasn't sure if her sudden arousal was because she was lying next to me in the quiet hotel room and she felt attracted to me, or if it was simply her teenage hormones taking control. Either way, there was no way I was going to be able to get back to sleep after that, and I waited until I heard her breathing returning to normal and she rolled over in her bed.

When I was sure she'd fallen back to sleep, I pulled down my panties and began jilling myself in furious circles over my burning clit. After getting so worked up listening to her touching herself, it didn't long for me to reach the peak of my pleasure. I bit my lip trying to stifle my groans as my body began convulsing in rhythmic contractions with my hand pressed tightly between my legs. When I finally stopped coming, I tried to control my breathing so as not to wake Brooke up. But when she suddenly rolled over again, I wondered if it was because she was restless or because she'd been listening to me the whole time.

Either way, I knew we'd both passed an important milestone in our mutual journey of discovery.

3

In the morning, Brooke woke up before me and went into the washroom to brush her teeth. My panties were still damp from my late-night masturbation session, and I was eager to get myself cleaned up before heading out. I sat up on the edge of my bed to check my messages, but it was all a blur as my mind raced thinking about what to do next. I couldn't bear the idea of leaving Brooke, but I had my life in Chicago and she was dead-set on traveling to LA. As I contemplated how to reconcile my conflicting urges, she stepped out of the washroom and paused in the doorway.

"Did you sleep well?" she asked.

I peered up, seeing the raised bumps of her areolas protruding atop her perky breasts under her braless tank top.

"Um, yes thank you," I stammered, momentarily taken aback by her sexy Elizabeth Taylor pose. "How about you?"

"Better than I have in a long time. Must be all this fresh midwestern air."

"That, or us staying up so late. What time do you figure we nodded off?"

"I dunno, but I enjoyed chatting with you into the wee hours. I haven't had that much fun since my grade school sleepovers."

"Everything but the pillow fight," I chuckled, alluding to our silent late-night tryst.

"Mmm," she nodded, flushing slightly.

I stood up and picked my toiletry bag out of my suitcase lying on the bench at the base of my bed.

"I need a shower. You'll probably want one too before heading back out on the road. You don't know when you might have the next opportunity. Do you want to go first?"

Brooke peered at my full breasts pressing against the flimsy cotton of my t-shirt. They were bigger than hers, and my erect nipples poked two sensuous darts in the light fabric. As I approached her near the entrance to the bathroom, she peered into my eyes and we hesitated for a moment. I was tempted to lean in and kiss her, but it still felt too soon. Besides, I didn't know if I was ever going to see her again. The last thing I needed was to get my pheromones all worked up again, only to be dashed when she sailed off into the sunset.

"No," she said, feeling our breasts only inches apart in the narrow doorway. "You go first. I'm going to check the highway route map to see the best place to pick up on my journey."

"Mmm," I nodded, not wanting to broach the subject that was on both of our minds. I could tell that neither of us was in any hurry to separate, but we were both painfully aware of the reality of the situation.

I continued into the washroom, closing the door partway behind me. Then I stepped out of my panties and pulled off my t-shirt, bending over to adjust the shower temperature. When I stood up to step into the tub, I caught Brooke peeking at me through the narrow crack, and she quickly turned away, pretending to thumb through her phone.

As I stepped into the warm shower feeling the soft spray caressing my bare tits and stomach, I flashed back to the scene from last night. Remembering the way Brooke raised her hips off the mattress and mewed when she came made my pussy tingle, and I snaked my hand between my legs and began to play with my nub. Within seconds, I had another powerful orgasm as I jerked and panted, trying to support myself with one hand against the slippery wall. When I finished washing my hair and cleaning my body, I stepped out of the tub and wrapped a towel around my torso and another around my wet hair. Then I opened the door as a rush of warm humid air spilled into the bedroom.

"Your turn," I said, smiling at Brooke. "I hope you don't mind that I took a couple of towels. There's still one large bath towel and a hand towel for you to use. You can borrow my hair dryer if you forgot to pack one."

"Thanks," Brooke said, slipping past me into the washroom. "Do you mind if I leave the door slightly ajar so as not to steam up the mirror?"

"I was thinking exactly the same thing," I smiled back at her.

Brooke closed the door partway then I heard the rustling of clothes as she disrobed, followed by the sound of the shower curtain being pulled back. When I heard the spray turn on, I peered up and saw her naked body briefly exposed in the mirror over the sink from my angle on the bed. Her tits were soft and round, like two bowls of Jello resting high on her chest, with pointy nipples that danced in the warm spray.

Oh, to be eighteen years old again, I thought as my pussy pulsed in unconscious spasms.

When she got out of the shower, she wrapped the bath sheet around her body and we took turns drying our hair with my blow dryer. Brooke left hers purposely damp to let it dry with a natural curl, and when she emerged from the bathroom, she reminded me of Kristen Stewart in the famous river scene from the finale of the Breaking Dawn Twilight movie. We got dressed separately in the privacy of the washroom, then we headed downstairs for a quick breakfast in the hotel restaurant before checking out.

After collecting a plateful of bacon and eggs from the breakfast bar, we sat down at our table and ate quietly together. Neither one of us wanted to acknowledge the elephant in the room. After a couple of minutes of awkward silence, I put my fork down on my plate and peered up at Brooke.

"Listen," I said. "I've been thinking. There's nothing urgent I need to rush home to for a few more days. Why don't I take you a little further along the way toward your destination? We can make a little adventure of it. Stop at Mount Rushmore, see the Grand Canyon, stuff like that."

"Like *Thelma and Louise*?!" she said, her eyes suddenly widening in excitement.

"Yes, everything except the driving over the cliff part at the end. That is, if you don't mind being seen in an *old person* car."

"I dunno," Brooke grinned. "It's a far cry from the Thunderbird convertible that Louise drove. But hey, beggars can't be choosers."

I lifted my glass of orange juice off the table and pointed it toward Brooke.

"Here's to new adventures," I said.

"To new adventures," she nodded, clinking her glass against mine.

After we packed our bags in the back of my SUV, Brooke turned toward me and wrapped her arms around my neck, giving me a bear hug.

"Thanks, Jade," she said. "I couldn't bear the idea of going the rest of the way without you. I feel like I've known you my whole life after being with you for only one day."

"Don't get your hopes up *too* far, young lady," I smiled. "I didn't promise to drive you the whole way. We'll take it day by day and see how far we can make it without getting into another fight."

"*Deal*," Brooke said, clapping her hands together excitedly.

We jumped in the car and after reaching the outskirts of Des Moines, I pulled back onto I-80 West, before angling northward toward Sioux Falls in South Dakota. We marveled at the passing landscape as the highway wound its way along the banks of the Missouri River, singing country songs the entire way while our hair flapped in the wind outside our open windows.

When we got to Mount Rushmore, we picnicked in the grass at the base of the mountain, then took selfies with the four presidents peering over our shoulder. I mimicked the serious expressions of Lincoln, Jefferson, Washington, and Roosevelt, while Brooke made funny faces, sticking her tongue out the side of her mouth as she rolled her eyes. I hadn't laughed and had so much fun for as long as I could remember, and for the first time in ages, I lost track of what day of the week it was. We were just following our noses, letting the car take us wherever it wanted as we pointed west.

I felt my heart soaring with every new mile we traveled, feeling closer and closer to this free-spirited girl. But it was more than just a strong friendship. I lusted to be in Brooke's arms, to feel her body pressed against mine as I ravished her and we pleasured each other to new heights. After our silent tryst the night before, I was afraid to make the next move, not knowing if she was ready for an intimate relationship with a woman.

As we continued across the midwestern plains into Wyoming, Brooke seemed to become more and more restless and she began to shift in her seat distractedly. Suddenly, she popped open the glove box and reached inside.

"Have you got any *good reading* material in here?" she said. "There's only so many cornfields a girl can watch before she needs a diversion."

"Um—not really," I hesitated, remembering something *else* I kept stored in the stowage compartment.

Brooke felt something hard with her hand and began pulling it out of the box.

"What's this?" she said. "Do you keep a gun in here, just like Louise? Were you planning on running into some dangerous characters along the way?"

"Ah—" I stammered, unsure how to stop her.

"*Holy shit!*" she said, holding up my special vibrator that I carried to keep me amused on long trips. "Is this what I *think* it is?"

"Um..."

"It *is!*" Brooke squealed, squeezing the soft silicone covering. "But I've never seen one like this before. Why is it shaped like a horseshoe?"

"It's a special type of vibrator," I smiled. "One that stimulates you on the inside and the outside at the same time."

"Really?" Brooke hummed. "You actually *use* this thing sometimes when you're driving?"

"Only when I'm especially bored or I feel drowsy on long trips. It certainly keeps me awake."

"I can imagine," Brooke said, gently flexing the two sides of the U-shaped device. "I've never used one like this before."

I smiled, happy to know she'd had a little experience using vibrators.

"You haven't *lived* until you've tried this one. You said you were looking for a distraction. Why don't you give it a try?"

"What–right *here*? Right *now*?"

"Why not? It's just us girls. No one will be able to see what you're doing this far under the windowsill."

"Except *you*. You're sitting right next to me."

"I promise not to look if you don't want me to. Besides, I need to keep my eyes on the road."

"Um," Brooke hesitated, beginning to squirm in her seat.

I could tell she was curious about giving it a try, but her modesty was holding her back.

"Here," I said, reaching into the back seat to retrieve her small travel bag. "Why don't you rest this on the console between the two of us. That will give you a certain degree of privacy. I won't be able to see much below your upper body that way. If you insist on being discreet."

Brooke hesitated for a moment, then peered over her shoulder into the back seat.

"I can't believe I'm actually thinking of doing this. But now you've piqued my curiosity."

"You could always wait until later tonight when the lights are out in our hotel room," I smiled.

"Very funny," Brooke grinned back at me. "I think I'll try

it here. I'm going to enjoy teasing you while your hands are tied up on the wheel. No peeking though, okay?

"I promise," I said. "Not unless you want me to."

Brooke lifted her travel bag between the two front seats and placed it on the dividing console. It wedged snugly between the two seats, and the gearshift kept it from sliding forward.

"Okay," Brooke said, peering over the top of the bag at me. "No cheating."

"Yes ma'am," I said, squeezing the steering wheel so tightly in anticipation that my fingers began to turn red.

Brooke reached down with her hands and wiggled her hips as she pulled her cut-off shorts and panties down around her ankles. Then she lifted up the U-shaped vibrator and peered at it curiously.

"Which end goes *inside*?"

"The fat end that's curved like a finger. I think you'll find it does quite a nice job of stimulating your G-spot. Then you place the narrower, flat end against your mound and push it all the way inside until it rests against your vulva. Do you need some *lube*? There's a small jar inside the glove–"

"No need," Brooke smiled. "I'm plenty lubricated already."

She spread her legs, and I saw the muscles of her arms tense as she pressed the device slowly inside her with two hands. She purred softly, then gasped when the soft outer tip rolled over her clitoris.

"Mmm–it feels heavenly," she purred. "But how do I turn it on?"

"That's the most fun part," I said, grinning back at her. "If you reach into the glove box, you'll find a separate attachment in the shape of a pink disk. It's a remote controller–so you can use it completely hands free."

Brooke placed her hand into the glove box and pulled out the strange-looking device, rubbing her fingers over the various indentations.

"There's a lot of buttons and switches on this thing," she said. "Which button controls which part?"

"You know what would be even *more* fun," I grinned. "Is if you let *me* operate the controls. That way, you can just put your head back and enjoy the ride."

"But I thought you said you needed to keep your eyes on the road?!"

"Oh, I can operate these controls entirely by *feel*, believe me. I've had plenty of practice."

"Okay," Brooke said, slowly handing me the controller overtop of the console. "But if I tell you to slow down or stop, you have to follow my instructions. I don't want you giving me a seizure or something."

"I wouldn't think of it," I smiled. "Are you ready?"

"I guess so," she said, tilting the back of her seat down a few inches and closing her eyes.

I tapped the lower control button once and I heard the vibrator begin to hum inside Brooke's pussy. She groaned as she wedged her body further down the seat, spreading her legs wider apart. I smiled, knowing the internal finger had begun to move slowly inside her.

"Good so far?" I said.

"Mmm, yes," she said, squirming in her seat. "More, please."

I tapped the lower button two more times, and the speed and motion of the internal wand ramped up in intensity.

Brooke groaned softly as her right hand gripped the handle on the side of her door.

"You *like*?" I said.

"Oh yes–very much," she mewed, beginning to move her

hips in rhythmic circles on the leather seat. "But what about the *outside* part? I can't feel it moving yet."

"Are you sure you can handle it?" I teased.

"*Fuck* yes," she groaned. "I need you to stimulate my clit."

I squeezed my legs together in my tight jeans, getting increasingly turned on by the sights and sounds of Brooke's mounting arousal. I gripped the disk tightly in my right hand while trying to keep my eyes glued ahead, but my vision kept drifting to my right the more worked up Brooke became.

"Okay," I said. "Here goes."

I tapped the upper button on the controller, then I heard a higher-pitched sound as the clitoral vibrator began to buzz against Brooke's mound.

"Oh *God*," Brooke moaned, gripping the door handle more tightly. "That feels incredible."

I glanced over at her upper body and saw her chest beginning to rise and fall as her breathing became more ragged. Suddenly I wished she'd chosen to go braless again under her tight tank top as I flashed back to the memory of her pretty tits pressing against the soft fabric.

"Mmm," I encouraged her, rubbing my thighs tighter together, feeling the seam of my crotch pulling up harder against my throbbing button.

"Do you want more?" I asked, peering over at her.

"There's *more*?" she said, looking at me incredulously.

"I can turn up the speed a bit higher if you think you can take it."

"Oh, I can *take* it, alright," Brooke panted.

I tapped the upper button twice more, and the clitoral vibrator began buzzing at a higher pitch and faster intensity.

"*Uhnn*," Brooke groaned, shifting further down in her

seat and spreading her legs further apart until her knees pressed against the sides of the footwell.

"Damn," she grunted. "I can't take this much longer. You're enjoying tormenting me, aren't you?"

"You have *no* idea," I purred, feeling my own pleasure rising from the friction of my seam against my burning clit.

"Oh God," she suddenly panted. "I'm gonna cum. I'm gonna come so hard–"

She lurched forward, jerking her torso in rhythmic movements as her legs flapped rapidly in and out.

"Oh *fuckkk*!" she hissed. "I'm cumming, Jade! *Uhnnn...*"

As I watched Brooke spasming in her seat from her powerful climax, a switch suddenly flipped in my body, and I grunted softly as my own silent orgasm washed over me. I was oblivious to the traffic rolling past us in both directions as my vision blurred from the intense pleasure I was feeling, knowing the two of us had achieved a new level of intimacy in our rapidly blossoming relationship.

I smiled, realizing this was another unexpected turn in our open-ended adventure.

4

After Brooke came down from her climax, she wiped down the vibrator then placed it back in the glove box. I was hoping she'd play with it a little longer or dare me to use it while I was driving, but it was starting to get late and we needed to find a place to put in for the night. Hotels were scarce in the eastern part of Wyoming, so we pulled into a run-down motel and I booked another room with two double beds.

After checking for any sign of bedbugs, I told Brooke to make herself comfortable while I searched for some takeout food. I had to drive ten more miles to find a fast-food outlet in the nearest town, and after picking up a bucket of fried chicken, I stopped off at the liquor store to buy a bottle of wine. I hoped that one or two glasses in the privacy of our own room might loosen Brooke's inhibitions about taking our relationship to the next level.

But when I stepped into the store, I immediately felt uncomfortable, surrounded by a bunch of middle-aged truckers and noisy rednecks wearing dirty baseball caps and greasy mullets. They leered at me as I stepped into the checkout line, and I was happy to get out of there and back to the relative safety of our little motor hotel.

But when I pulled into the parking lot, I saw Brooke standing outside our door flanked by two young men who were pushing her against the wall, trying to grope her. I could tell from the look in her eyes that she was frightened, and I screeched the brakes, pulling up directly in front of them.

"*Hey!*" I yelled, swinging my car door open and grabbing the paper bag with the bottle of wine. "*Get away from her!*"

"Who's this?" one of the punks said, gripping Brooke's arm while he pressed his face closer to hers. "Is this your Mommy coming to save you from the big bad wolf?"

Brooke shook her head apprehensively while pressing herself further back against the wall.

"What do you want, *bitch*?" the boy said, teetering unsteadily and obviously drunk. "Can't you see I'm busy? Why don't you mind your own business and lose yourself in your bottle of wine? Or better yet, share it with *us*."

As he lurched toward me, without thinking, I coiled back and gave him a hard kick to the side of his knee. He howled in pain from the torn ligament and crumpled to the ground. His friend stepped toward me threateningly, and I crashed the end of the bottle against my side mirror as wine spilled out onto the pavement and jagged glass jutted out the end of the torn bag.

"You want some of this too?" I scowled, pressing the sharp glass up close to his face. "I won't hesitate to cut you up like a tree chipper if you get any closer."

The boy looked at me for a moment, then peered down at his fallen comrade, still squirming in pain on the ground.

"Come on, Bo," he said, reaching down to help him off the pavement. "This bitch is bat-shit crazy, and that tramp ain't worth it. Let's get the hell out of here before someone calls the cops."

The boy on the ground staggered to his feet and began limping away, when I noticed a bulge in the back pocket of his jeans. I reached in and pulled out his wallet, flipping through the contents.

"What the *fuck*?" the boy said. "Give me back my wallet or I'll call the cops!"

I pulled out his driver's license, then threw his wallet back down on the ground.

"You can *have* your wallet," I said. "But I'm keeping your ID in case you two get any ideas about coming back here anytime soon. Feel free to call the police. We'll see who gets taken to the station house. I'll leave your license at the front desk when I check-out. Now get the fuck out of here!"

The injured boy placed his arm over his friend's shoulder then they limped to the other side of the parking lot and got into an old Camaro, squealing their tires out of the compound.

Brooke peeled herself off the wall and looked at me incredulously.

"Holy shit, Jade!" she said. "That was *bad-ass!* Where did you learn those moves?"

"Just reflex, I guess. The adrenaline was pumping pretty hard when I saw what they were doing to you. Are you alright?"

"Yes," she said. "It's mostly just my pride that was injured." She peered down at the broken bag of wine, still dripping onto the blacktop. "It's a good thing you brought that bottle of wine. That scared them away right quick!"

"Sorry," I said, throwing the bag into a trash receptacle near our door. "I was hoping we could share a little together to celebrate reaching your halfway point."

"No worries," Brooke said. "There'll be plenty more opportunities along the way. Did you pick up some food? I've been starved since our picnic earlier in the day."

I opened the rear driver's side door and pulled out the bag of KFC.

"Fried chicken," I smiled. "Your favorite!"

We went inside the cabin and spread a towel over one of the beds, then we sat cross-legged on the mattress facing one another while Brooke replayed the scene outside.

"What were you *thinking*?" I said, peering at her with pinched eyebrows. "What prompted you to leave the room?"

"I just wanted to get a soda from the pop machine near the lobby. I didn't see the two goons until it was too late."

"It's okay, babe," I said, placing my hand on her still-quivering shoulder. "You've got to be careful out there. Like I said, there's a lot of scary people just waiting to take advantage of a single girl like you."

"Don't worry," she smiled guiltily. "I'm not going *anywhere* without you from now on."

After we finished eating and cleaning up in the washroom, I peered at Brooke and smiled.

"Are you ready to turn in? It's getting pretty late. Do you think you'll be able to sleep after all this?"

Brooke stood next to her bed with her arms crossed tightly over her chest, still shaking visibly.

"Do you mind if I sleep with you tonight?" she said. "I'll feel safer having a warm body next to me."

"Of course," I smiled, turning down the covers of my bed. "There should be enough room for the two of us."

As I pulled off my jeans and draped them over the back of the chair, Brooke stepped out of her cut-off shorts and threw them on top of the opposite bed.

"You might want to put those somewhere *else*," I said. "I'm guessing that bedspread hasn't been washed in months. You never know what kind of germs might be lurking in this place."

"Right," she said, lifting her shorts off the bed and placing them atop my jeans on the back of the chair. Then she pulled her bra down under her shirt and placed it cup-side-up on top of her shorts. I followed suit, then we both lay down on the bed wearing only our cotton shirts and panties.

After I turned out the night table lamp, Brooke nestled in closer to me, squeezing her body against mine.

"Thanks, Jade," she whispered in my ear. "I feel so lucky to have found you. And not just because you saved me today. There's something else. I've never felt this way with–"

I placed my hand at the side of her head and pulled her face into mine, kissing her gently. She mewed like a kitten while pressing her hips against me, grinding her mound against mine. I pulled her head harder toward me and slipped my tongue into her mouth, teasing the inside of her lips. She moaned as she wrapped her arms around my back, pressing her tits against mine.

I pulled back for a second and peered into her eyes in the faint light projected by the digital clock on the desk.

"Are you sure you want to do this?" I asked. "I don't want to take advantage–"

"I've been wanting you to make love to me ever since we had that fight in the restaurant. Haven't you felt the sexual tension too?"

"Yes," I said, kissing her softly. "I've just been looking for the right moment–"

Brooke leaned back a few inches and pulled off her tank top then threw it over her shoulder onto the opposite bed.

"Aren't you worried about the *germs*?" I said.

"Not *those* ones," she smiled. "I'm looking forward to intermingling with some *other* organisms."

"Mmm," I said, pulling off my t-shirt and throwing it on top of hers.

Brooke threw her arms around me, mashing her tits against mine as we moaned into each other's mouths. I could tell from her awkward movements that this was her first time with a woman, and I decided to go slow so as not to scare her away. Normally, I'd have started kissing my way down her body by now, sucking her teats and clit into my mouth as I indulged her with my more experienced skills. But right now, I just wanted to feel her body against mine while I kissed her sweet face. There'd be plenty more time to get down and dirty after a good night's sleep.

As the two of us intertwined our legs and began rubbing our pussies together, I could feel my panties getting wetter and wetter as the lacy fabric pulled and scratched against my skin. I reached down under the covers and began pulling Brooke's panties down over her hips, and she lifted her knees up and kicked them off her feet. I raised my hips off the mattress and did the same thing, pushing the two pairs of panties out of our way down toward the base of the bed. Then I pressed my knee between her legs and pulled my thigh up toward her crotch. I was surprised how wet she was already, and I groaned when I felt her warm pussy against the soft skin of my upper leg. As I began rocking my thigh over her dripping vulva, she sighed in my ear while nibbling my earlobe.

"Make love to me, Jade," she whispered. "I want to feel your body against mine while I listen to you in the dark again."

I pulled away and smiled into her eyes.

"So you *did* hear me last night after all?" I said, flaring my eyes in mock surprise.

"Of course," she said. "Did you hear me?"

"How could I *not*? With all that shuffling and heavy breathing, I knew immediately what you were up to."

"Did that turn you on?" she said.

"Damn straight," I said, rolling on top of her. "You have no idea how much I've fantasized about fucking you since then."

"Mmm," Brooke groaned, feeling my bare mound rubbing up against her soft muff. "Fuck me, Jade. I want to feel your juices dripping over my pussy."

"*God* yes," I panted, pressing her legs apart with my knees and positioning myself over her upper body as our sweaty tits slid effortlessly over one another.

Brooke tilted her hips up a few degrees until her clit made contact with the base of my mound, then she thrust her tongue into my mouth, groaning loudly as I rubbed her wet vulva. I loved the feel of her downy pubic hair against my belly, and as much as I wanted to bury my face in her pussy, there was something sweet and romantic about pressing our bodies together in the missionary style.

As I began rocking my hips back and forth against hers, I felt her hard button flapping against mine while I coated the insides of her thighs with my juices. Brooke dug her fingernails into my back as she pressed her pussy harder against mine with her breathing slowly ratcheting up in intensity.

"Yes, Jade," she grunted. "You feel so good."

"Even better than my vibrator?" I teased.

"Fuck, yes," she panted. "You're warm and soft, and *much more* responsive. *Come* with me, Jade. I'm getting close...."

"*Brooke*," I panted in her ear, feeling my pleasure rapidly spreading inside me. "I feel so close to you..."

"Uhnn," Brooke groaned, wrapping her legs tightly around my ass. "I'm cumming, Jade! Cum with me!"

Suddenly I felt the floodgates open as my hips began shaking over Brooke's steaming pussy. For the next thirty seconds, we bucked our hips wildly together, holding each other close and kissing each other passionately. My mind was swimming in delirious pleasure, not only because of the intense contractions emanating from between my legs, but because I knew Brooke and I had reached a new level of intimacy. I hadn't felt this close to anyone in a long time, and as we held each other tightly in the pitch dark, Brooke whispered in my ear that she loved me too.

5

Brooke and I fell asleep in each other's arms not long after, and when I awoke she was nestled with her back against my tummy. I reached around and caressed her breasts, and she purred softly. Then she turned her face toward me, and I kissed her gently.

"Mmm," she purred. "I could get used to this."

"Me too," I said, wrinkling my forehead as I peered into her eyes. "But I don't know how much longer we'll have a chance to be together like this."

She flipped over to face me and smiled, ignoring the black cloud that seemed poised to burst our bubble.

"We better get *busy* then," she said, rubbing her breasts playfully against mine. "You seem to have more experience with this sort of thing than I do. Teach me how to make love to a woman. I want to learn *everything* about you."

"It's not so different than you might expect," I said, temporarily forgetting my troubles as I nibbled my way down her neck. "Just do what comes naturally. You'll know when you're hitting the right buttons."

Brooke arched her back, lifting her chest to meet my face.

"Yes, Jade," she mewed. "Kiss my body all over. I want to learn how to please you like your other partners."

"*You're* the only partner I want right now," I said, rolling my tongue over her raised areolas, wondering how much sexual experience she'd actually had. "I love your pretty breasts. Have you ever been kissed like this before?"

"Never like *that*," she groaned. "Boys just go straight for my nipples and suck on them like they're inhaling a milkshake."

"The key is to go slow and *worship* a woman's body," I chuckled. "Girls are different from boys in the way they get aroused and experience sexual pleasure. It's not just about sticking it in and getting off. You have to *tease* your partner, build up her excitement, and let her enjoy the journey instead of focusing on the destination."

"Mmm, I like that metaphor," Brooke sighed as I squeezed her breasts while teasing the base of her nipples with little circles of my tongue. "This trip has exceeded my expectations in *so* many ways. I never expected to find my soulmate in the middle of the desert."

I could feel my heart beating faster and faster the more Brooke talked about how she felt about me, but I wasn't sure if it was because I shared similar feelings, or because I knew she'd soon be wrenched away from me. But at this moment, that was the last thing I wanted to think about. I just wanted to revel in her body and bring her to new heights of pleasure.

I pinched her nipples, feeling them harden between my fingers, then I placed my lips over one of her teats and sucked it like a lollypop, swirling my tongue around the edges as Brooke groaned in pleasure.

"*Jade*," she whispered. "I love the way you make love to me. I want to feel you caress *every* part of my body."

I smiled as Brooke's hips began to undulate in expectation against my belly while I kissed my way down the center of her stomach. When I reached her navel, I pressed my tongue inside her cavity and swirled it around the perimeter, foreshadowing what we both knew was soon to come.

"Uhnn," she moaned, lifting her hips off the bed and grinding her wet pussy against my breasts nestled between her thighs. I rocked my tits against her opening, feeling her juices coat me like maple syrup.

I nibbled my way further down her abdomen until I reached her soft muff, rolling my face over her downy fur. As much as I enjoyed a bare pussy, it was always a delight whenever I encountered a full patch of pubic hair, since it reminded me of my partner's innocence. Brooke was still too young and inexperienced to succumb to the societal pressure to trim her bush. I could taste her dewy sweetness on the tips of her hair, and as she rocked her pussy against the front of my neck, I smiled, knowing how much I was turning her on.

"*Lick me*, Jade," she begged. "I want to feel you kissing me the way you did last night."

"Mmm," I purred, lowering my face to her fragrant pussy, licking the sides of her slit while I tasted her honey.

The closer my tongue came to her opening, the wider she spread her knees, pulling my face closer to her snatch. I extended my tongue and pressed it inside her hole, and she groaned, gripping the sheets on either side of her hips.

"Oh God, Jade," she sighed. "Fuck me with your tongue. That feels so good."

I grinned, realizing this was a whole new experience for her, so different from the feeling of the plastic vibrator buzzing inside her yesterday. There was no substitute for a warm body lying next to a woman–licking, sucking, and caressing her body with her soft skin.

I gripped the sides of Brooke's hips with my hands and pulled her closer to me, burying my face in her sopping pussy. She began rocking her vulva faster and faster against my face, and I could tell from the pace of her breathing that she was going to come soon. But I wanted to feel her in my mouth when she came, and I pulled out of her hole and swiped my tongue up towards her apex like I was licking an ice cream cone. When I reached her flaring jewel, she gasped and threw her head back against the pillow.

"*Oh my God!*" she gasped. "This is *so* much better than a vibrator. I had no idea it could be this good."

"You've never been kissed down here before?" I said, peering up at her from under the covers.

"Nothing like this. The few boys I've been with never seem to be able to *find* it, let alone spend time pleasuring me there. They only seem interested in one thing. I had no idea how good this could feel."

"We've hardly just begun, baby," I said, encircling her gland with my lips, rolling my tongue over it gently.

"*Fuckkk*," Brooke hissed, pulling the undersheet up harder toward her. "Suck me, Jade. I want to come in your mouth."

"Mmm," I nodded, too busy teasing her clit to come up for air.

While Brooke slowly titled her hips toward me, I felt her buttock muscles clenching in my palms as I gripped her ass tightly. With her chest rising and falling in erratic gasps, her legs began to quiver, and I buried my nose in her dripping pubic hair as she began to lift her hips off the mattress.

"Jade," she squealed. "I'm going to cum. Oh God, I'm going to cum in your sweet mouth. Feel me Jade! Feel me–"

Suddenly, Brooke grabbed the back of my head and pulled me hard against her pussy while her hips began quaking against my face. I could feel her juices running down over my neck and tits as her pussy began spasming in powerful contractions.

"*Jade, Jade, Jade...*" she panted with each contraction. "I'm cumming. I'm cumming in your beautiful mouth."

Up to this point, I'd hardly paid any attention to my own pleasure while I concentrated on pleasing Brooke. But when I felt her shaking against my face and she began wailing in ecstasy, suddenly my own pussy pulsed in sympathy as I began gushing all over the sheets between my legs. I held her softly in my mouth until she stopped quivering, then I lifted my head and kissed her soft pubic patch, inhaling her heavenly aroma. Then I pulled myself up next to her and kissed her as we intermingled our tongues.

"Oh my God," she said when we finally pulled ourselves apart. "I've never been made love to like that before. That was the most beautiful, erotic, tender thing I've ever experienced."

"I'm glad you liked it baby," I smiled. "I felt exactly the same way. I like making love to you."

"What about *you* now?" she said, propping herself up on an elbow. "I want to learn how to please you the same way. I've been dreaming about licking you down there for two days..."

"There's still plenty of time for that," I said, pinning her back down onto the bed. "But this time I want to *see* you while I make love to you. No more hiding under the covers and rubbing our bodies together in the dark."

"I like the sound of that," Brooke smiled. "But when do *I* get to be on top?"

"Maybe next time," I grinned, placing my ass over her pelvis. "You said you wanted me to teach you how to make love to a woman. Well this time, I'm gonna *fuck* you. Sometimes you want it soft and sometimes you want it hard. This time I want it *hard*."

"Fuck yes," Brooke hissed. "Fuck me, Jade. I want to look into your eyes while you fuck me."

"You're reading my mind, girl," I said. "Now lift up one knee and spread your legs."

"That sounds dirty–"

"Sometimes dirty is *good*," I smiled, straddling her extended leg and lowering my pussy toward her crotch.

When our vulvas touched, Brooke groaned and reached up to squeeze my tits.

"Mmm, yes," she purred. "I'm going to enjoy watching you fuck me. Plus, I get to play with *other* parts of you while we watch each other."

"Exactly," I said, pulling the underside of her raised leg against my stomach as I pressed my cunt hard against hers.

"Uhnn," Brooke whinnied, squeezing my tits tighter. "Your pussy's so wet."

"That's at least half *you*, girl," I grunted, pulling her tighter against me.

As we began to rock our hips together, Brooke reached out her hands to me, and I intertwined my fingers with hers, clasping her hands tightly.

"You're so beautiful," she said, peering at me with a sad expression. "I love watching you make love to me."

"You too, babe," I smiled, happy she was recognizing the distinction. Although I was fucking her in every sense of the word, at this moment, I felt closer to her than I ever had.

"I'm going to come soon, hun," I said, suddenly feeling overwhelmed with the sights and sounds of this sweet angel lying prone underneath me.

"Yes, Jade," Brooke said. "Let me watch you come while we're connected together."

I was surprised how quickly I'd reached the height of my passion, but there was something about the sight of my new lover peering up at me bittersweetly while squeezing my hands that put me over the edge. We both knew that we'd soon have to part company, and the thought of it tore us both apart.

As my body began quivering atop hers, a small tear streamed out of my eye and rolled down my cheek. No words were necessary between us as our bodies began shaking together and we peered into each other's eyes. After we came down from our climaxes, I slumped over onto her body, feeling her soft breath caressing the side of my ear. I didn't know how much longer I'd be with Brooke, but in this moment, I just wanted to hold her forever.

6

———

Brooke and I made love for the rest of the morning, then we got back in the car and headed south along I-25 toward Colorado and the Grand Canyon. As we marveled at the spectacular scenery of the snow-capped Rocky Mountains, neither of us was very talkative knowing we were getting ever-closer to the west coast where we'd have to part company. But after a half hour of pensively looking out her side window, Brooke suddenly laughed.

"What?" I asked.

"I was just thinking back to the incident outside our motel yesterday..."

"What was so funny about that?"

"*Wood chipper?*" she said, looking at me with a raised eyebrow.

"Huh?"

"When you said to that guy that was threatening you that you'd cut him up like a wood chipper if he got any closer."

I chuckled, realizing how ridiculous that sounded after the fact.

"It was the best I could think of in the heat of the moment."

"Well it sure worked," she said. "You scared the crap out of both of those guys."

"Well, good riddance," I said, peering over at Brooke. "Who needs *boys* anyway, right?"

"After last night," she smiled, "I can't imagine I'll ever want to turn back."

I gazed out my windscreen for the next few minutes, thinking about Brooke's future life. Was it really fair of me to steal her affections when she'd be leaving so soon? Was it even fair for me to try to turn her against boys her own age? She had her whole life ahead of her and there'd be so many new and exciting opportunities in California.

"Have you been thinking much about L.A. these past few days?" I said.

"A little bit," she said. "I'm a bit worried, to be honest. Being all alone, competing with all those beautiful people in Hollywood. Do you think I'll be able to make a go of it?"

I reached over the console and squeezed her hand gently.

"Well, since I met you, you've reminded me at different moments of Marilyn Monroe, Elizabeth Taylor, Geena Davis, and Kristen Stewart. I think you can hold your own against *anyone*. I wouldn't be surprised to see you on the big screen one day."

"Opposite *Robert Pattinson* maybe?" she said.

"Is that your leading man type?"

"Well, he *is* kind of dreamy," Brooke said. "Or maybe it was just that whole romantic premise of the Twilight story line."

"So you're saying you dig *vampires*?"

Brooke chuckled softly, then peered back outside her

window at the passing landscape. The road was almost devoid of cars as we rolled by the broad ranches of southern Wyoming. Suddenly, a lone figure appeared on the horizon, about a half a mile ahead of us on the side of the road. It appeared to be another hitchhiker. As we got closer, we saw that it was a young man wearing a cowboy hat and faded jeans. Brooke suddenly perked up, squinting through the windshield. When we passed by, we couldn't help noticing how handsome he was.

Brooke turned to look at me with wide eyes.

"Did you *see* that?" she said.

"Uh-huh. He was kind of cute, wasn't he?"

"Cute?" she said. "That was one sexy-ass cowboy."

"Well he's no Brad Pitt. But I suppose he'd do in a pinch."

"Aren't you going to *stop*?" she said, furrowing her brow like a sad puppy dog.

I took my foot off the gas pedal for a moment, considering her request. As much as I wanted to have Brooke for myself the rest of the trip, I knew this would be the perfect opportunity to wean her off me and begin making some new friends with people her own age.

I peered back at her and smiled as I pulled off the road. Then I honked my horn twice and began to back up along the shoulder. I had no idea where the boy was headed or how long he'd stay with us, but something told me the sparks were about to fly once again with my pretty, young wayfarer.

Everybody's an exhibitionist in disguise...

Spying on the neighbors just got a lot more interesting...

Sometimes you need to talk through your problems to lose your inhibitions...

PEEP SHOW

VICTORIA RUSH

Nothing's more exciting than knowing you're being watched...

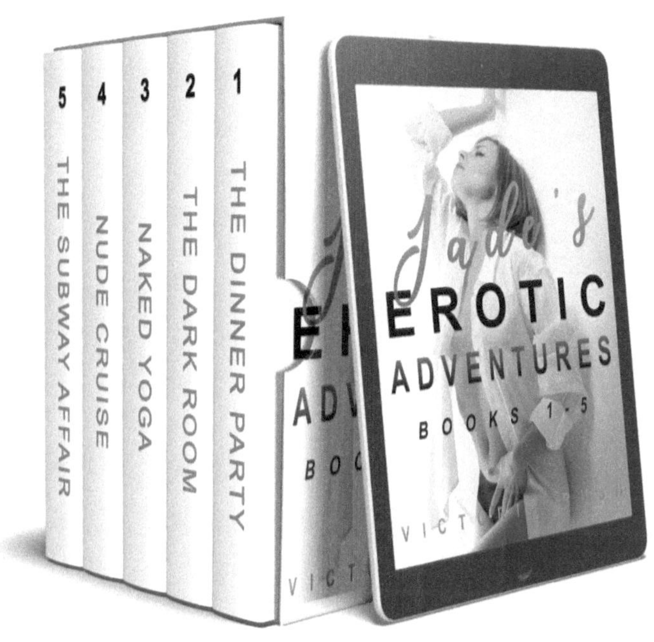

Books 1 -5 in the bestselling erotica series - 60% off

"Every time I see you, I want to tell one of those bad gynecologist jokes," I said to my sex therapist friend Hannah at our weekly luncheon.

Hannah rolled her eyes as she took another bite of her salad. Her practice seemed to be the never-ending butt of jokes among our friends, but she'd learned to take the digs with good humor.

"Well you know I'm a far cry from a gynecologist, but I could use a little laugh today, so if you really need to get it out of your system, lay it on me."

"Ok, so this old lady goes to see her dentist," I started. "When her appointment is called, she sits in the chair, lowers her underpants, and raises her legs..."

"Uh huh," Hannah murmured, lifting a glass of soda water to her lips to signal her disinterest.

"So the dentist says," I continued, 'Excuse me, but I'm not a gynecologist.'"

I paused long enough for Hannah to begin swallowing her water. "'I know,' said the old lady. 'I want you to take my husband's teeth out.'"

Hannah lurched forward, spewing her soda water all over her salad as she raised her hand to her mouth, coughing loudly.

"Are you okay?" I said, glancing at the surrounding restaurant patrons alarmed by the sudden commotion at our table.

"Y–yeah," Hannah gagged. "The water just went down the wrong way. I wasn't expecting that punchline."

"Pretty good, right?" I smiled.

"Better than most, I'll grant you," she nodded. "But I don't know why you guys always make fun of my practice. *Someone* has to help all the sexually dysfunctional people out there."

"I know," I said, frowning sheepishly. "It's just hard to imagine what goes on in your office when people talk candidly about their sex lives."

"You'd be surprised," Hannah said, taking another swig of water to clear her throat. "In fact, I was thinking of inviting you to one of my sessions sometime."

I pinched my eyebrows and shook my head, surprised at her offer.

"As a *patient* or as an observer?"

"You don't need any help with your sex life," she said.

"You're already miles ahead of me with all your wild escapades and adventures. I'd like to present you as more of a role model for what a healthy, sexually uninhibited person looks like."

"What would you have me *do* exactly? Don't you have to protect patient-doctor privilege? I thought you guys had to keep everything at arms-length, so to speak."

"I've been experimenting with some different strategies lately," Hannah smiled. "Let's just say I've been trying out some more *active* therapeutic techniques."

"No way!" I said, widening my eyes as I rested my cocktail on the table so as not to spill it. "Isn't that against the rules? I thought you had to maintain a certain degree of professional distance or risk losing your license."

"I still do. The only difference is now I encourage them to practice some of the prescribed self-empowerment techniques in my *office* instead of at home, so I can coach and guide them more actively. Besides, everybody signs a waiver before we take it to the next level."

"Holy shit!" I said, shaking my glass incredulously. "While you *watch* them touch themselves intimately?"

"Sometimes," Hannah nodded. "But most patients prefer to be concealed behind a protective screen when they first start the process."

"So you basically guide them through a facilitated *masturbation* session?"

"In a manner of speaking, yes. I find most patients need a little more active engagement to get them over the hump becoming comfortable enjoying sex with another person. You'd be surprised how many sexually dysfunctional women there are out there."

"So most of your patients are women?"

"Yes—I find them much more interesting to work with."

"Oh my God," I panted, beginning to feel my panties moisten under my tight jeans. "I'd love to be a fly on the wall in one of these sessions. How do you manage to stay focused when things start to heat up? Don't you get aroused while these women pleasure themselves?"

Hannah shifted uncomfortably in her chair, signaling for the waiter to bring her another cocktail.

"I do. At first, I just kind of squirmed in my chair and squeezed my legs together in frustration. But I've discovered a more animated way to keep myself stimulated while I watch my patients enjoying themselves."

My eyes flew open as the fluid in my cocktail glass began to tremble.

"You stick a *vibrator* down your pants?!" I said. "Isn't that kind of noisy? How do you hide that from your patients?"

"It's not just *any* vibrator," Hannah said with a crooked grin. "Our friend Cheryl from the local Babeland store introduced me to a new kind of toy. It's designed by a woman to mimic the touch and movement of real fingers and lips. It doesn't buzz so much as *hum* as it undulates both inside and on the outside of your vulva."

"Jesus!" I squealed, furrowing my brow in frustration. "Just when I thought I had the full collection of the latest toys. What does this thing look like?"

Hannah opened up her purse and passed me a large finger-shaped device attached to a hollow cone at the base.

"I just happen to carry one with me wherever I go," she said. "See for yourself."

I peered at the strange-looking object, stroking the soft silicone surface gently.

"It sure doesn't look like anything I've seen before. How does it work if it doesn't vibrate?"

"The long finger-shaped appendage goes inside you and

bends in a series of come-hither motions against your G-spot. Give it a try by tapping the control button on the base one time."

I pressed the button and the finger began waving toward me like some kind of animatronic alien finger.

"*What the fuck*?" I said. "That's insane! It moves just like a real finger. And it hardly makes a sound."

"That the best part. You can use it anywhere. Even in a crowded restaurant. You should give it a try. Pretend that you're reclining on a couch in my office."

I glanced around the table to make sure no one else had seen the strange device that I was fondling at the table.

"It's tempting," I said, peering into the orifice at the top of the cone. "But what's with this little hole near the bottom of the device? What goes on there?"

"See for yourself," Hannah smiled. "Tap the button a second time. You might be in for a bit of a surprise."

I tapped the button again and a long, tongue-shaped object pushed up out of the hole and began undulating like a hypnotic snake against my palm.

My eyes grew wide as saucers as Hannah nodded at me with a huge smirk.

"Like I said," she grinned. "It's not a vibrator so much as a *replicator*. Doesn't it remind you of a real finger and tongue?"

"In a weird, perverted, *ET* kind of way–yeah."

Hannah lowered her gaze and nodded toward my midsection.

"You've got to feel it down there to really appreciate it. Go ahead–give it a try. No one needs to know besides us girls."

"Seriously?" I said. "Right here?!"

"Why not? There's a long skirt surrounding the table.

You can loosen your pants and insert it inside you without anyone knowing. Let me have a little bit of fun watching you pleasure yourself for a change. We haven't been together that way in quite a while."

"I have to admit," I huffed. "I *am* insanely horny right now. I'm dying to try this thing out. But what are you going to do while I amuse myself?"

"I'm going to eat my salad like we're having a normal luncheon. This is all about *you* girl, don't worry about me. Knock yourself out."

"I can't believe I'm thinking about doing this," I said, watching the tongue slither back into its hole as I turned the toy off temporarily.

"It should be pretty easy to insert it if you're already properly worked up," Hannah said, lifting her glass to her lips.

I glanced to both sides of our table to make sure nobody else was watching, then reached under the tablecloth and unzipped my jeans, pulling them down to the floor. I could feel my juices already pooling on the wooden chair between my legs as I lowered the device under the table.

"Just be sure to position it so the hole is over your clit," Hannah whispered.

"I'm all over that," I nodded, slowly inserting the bulbous tip into my opening.

It slipped inside my slit smoothly, and I gasped as I pushed it all the way up inside me.

"It's not like just *any* old finger, is it?" Hannah grinned.

"No," I panted. "It's longer and fatter than most."

"It's designed with the ideal shape and form to stimulate your G-spot. If you've got it pressed all the way inside, turn it on to see what it feels like when it's animated."

I glanced around me nervously, watching the other restaurant patrons lost in conversation with their partners.

"Are you sure I'm going to be able to control myself in full view of all these customers? What if I break out into a Meg Ryan in front of all these people?"

"That'll be up to you to keep things under control as much as you can. But if not, what's the worst that can happen? Just like in the movie, everybody will want to know what you ordered that made you so happy."

"Very funny," I said, fumbling to find the control button on the base of the unit resting over my mound.

I pressed the button and began squirming in my chair as the long pointed finger began caressing me like no lover I ever had.

"Uhnn," I groaned, feeling the unusual stimulation inside my pussy.

"Not too bad, is it?" Hannah smiled. "Imagine all that going on while you're watching one of my patients pleasuring themselves."

"Is that really *possible*?" I said, getting even more turned on at the thought of watching one of her clients playing with herself in Hannah's private office.

"I've been thinking about it for a while," Hannah nodded. "It's the logical next step in the process of learning to become fully functional in a paired relationship. I've already had a few of my patients suggest they'd like me to guide them through their first encounter with another partner."

"You know how I like to *watch*," I groaned, as my eyes began to glaze over from the delicate sensation of the long finger rubbing up against my G-spot.

Hannah crossed her legs under the table and began to

bob up and down as she flexed her buttocks and thighs together watching me get off.

"I do," she said, lifting her cocktail glass off the table and sliding her tongue around the rim suggestively. "Try the tongue action now."

"You're such a tease," I hissed, reaching under the table-cloth and tapping the control button one more time.

When I felt the flexible appendage push out of the hole and begin rolling over my hard clit, I bent over my place setting, grasping the handles of my chair tightly.

"That's it, babe," Hannah purred. "Feel the rhythm. Close your eyes and imagine it's your fantasy partner licking your pussy. Surrender to the feeling..."

"Is this how you do it with your clients?" I panted. "Talking to them all sexy while they play with themselves?"

"Sometimes," Hannah smiled. "Or sometimes I just let them do most of the vocalization while they tell me what they're doing behind the screen."

I spread my knees further apart imagining myself in one of her sessions.

"Do they ever get to the point where they're comfortable letting you watch them?"

"That's the ultimate goal. I've had a number of clients reach that level already. But I'd like to try taking it one step further. That's where you come in–"

"Tell me, Han," I moaned, beginning to lose myself in the fantasy. "Tell me what you want me to do with your sexy patients."

"We'll start out slowly at first," she instructed. "We'll just have you listen to them moan and purr as they begin the process of self-discovery behind the safety of their protective screen. But you'll have to be quiet at first to not distract their self-focus."

"At *this* point," I said, beginning to feel the pleasure spreading over my entire body. "That might be enough. With this amazing device doing its thing, I could probably get off listening to the sound of running water."

"That's the intent," Hannah laughed. "At least for my clients. But in order for them to become truly uninhibited and be able to function competently, the next step would be for the two of you to emerge from your hiding places and become comfortable watching each other in a face-to-face setting."

"*Fuck, yes*," I panted. "If I can help another soul learn to enjoy the full pleasures of lesbian sex, count me in!"

"I know *you* won't have any trouble participating in this next phase of the process," Hannah smiled. "Just try to keep some of your more extreme methods in check for a while so you don't scare away my customers."

"I promise to keep my big dildos at home if you insist," I smirked.

"Once we get them feeling comfortable touching themselves and achieving climax in this voyeur scenario, the last step will be for the two of you to join together on the same couch and explore each other with more direct contact."

"Can I break out some of my favorite moves then?"

"If you find your partner is responding appropriately. Just be careful to always be gentle and focused on her needs. If you get to the point where she feels comfortable getting more inventive, by all means–"

"Oh, I've got the *means* alright," I moaned, imaging myself straddling one of her patients with her legs splayed wide apart as we ground our pussies together and I watched her come all over me. "How soon can we set this up?"

"I've got a certain patient in mind. She's young and never been with another woman before. She's had some unfulfilling experiences with men and confided that she's always fantasized about being with a woman. We'll just have to ease her into it carefully. Are you up for the opportunity, assuming she's game?"

"You know I am," I grunted, pressing harder down against the artificial tongue. "But first, tell me more about this girl..."

"She's nineteen, a sophomore in college, with a cheer-leader's body–"

"She's athletic then?"

"Oh yes," Hannah smiled. "Tight ass, firm tits, and legs that could wrap all the way around you while you tribbed her virgin pussy–"

"Oh God, Han," I moaned. "I can't take it any longer. Sign me up–I want to taste her sweet pussy in my mouth..."

"Yes, Jade," Hannah purred. "Let it go, hun. Surrender to the feeling–"

As I imagined the co-ed writhing in ecstasy sitting on my face, the pleasure generated by the lifelike sex toy suddenly peaked, and I bit my lip as I began convulsing in my chair. I'd never fought so hard to remain quiet during a powerful orgasm in my entire life. There was something about the experience of cumming surrounded by scores of oblivious restaurant patrons that made the experience all the more erotic. While I twisted and squirmed in my chair, Hannah smiled as she raised her glass in toast to me.

"Congratulations, Jade," she said. "You've just passed the first test with flying colors."

READ MORE...

If you would like to receive notification of new book(s) in Jade's Erotic Adventures, follow me at http://bookbub.com/authors/victoria-rush.

If you have a moment, please post a brief review on my Amazon book page at viewbook.at/thehitchhiker . Even just a couple of sentences will help other readers find and enjoy this book as much as you hopefully did.

Follow, share, like, and comment at:

www.facebook.com/authorvictoriarush
www.pinterest.com/authorvictoriarush
www.twitter.com/authorvictoriarush
authorvictoriarush@outlook.com

Hope to see you again soon!

www.ingramcontent.com/pod-product-compliance
Lightning Source LLC
Chambersburg PA
CBHW030822200726
48288CB00004B/1350